A little fawn-coloured reindeer
with white patches came out of
the trailer on wobbly legs. Her
antlers were so tiny, they were
even smaller than her ears!

Look out for:

The Runaway Reindeer

Amelia Cobb

Illustrated by
Sophy Williams

nosy
crow

With special thanks to Siobhan Curham

For Sadie Hardin

First published in the UK in 2021 by Nosy Crow Ltd
The Crow's Nest, 14 Baden Place
Crosby Row, London SE1 1YW

www.nosycrow.com

ISBN: 978 1 78800 937 9

Nosy Crow and associated logos are trademarks and/or
registered trademarks of Nosy Crow Ltd

Text copyright © Working Partners Ltd, 2021
Illustrations © Sophy Williams, 2021

The right of Working Partners Ltd and Sophy Williams to be identified as the author
and illustrator respectively of this work has been asserted by them in accordance with the
Copyright, Designs and Patents Act 1988.

A CIP catalogue record for this book will be available from the British Library

Printed and bound in Great Britain by Clays Ltd, Elcograf S.p.A.

Papers used by Nosy Crow are made from wood grown in sustainable forests.

1 3 5 7 9 10 8 6 4 2

Chapter One
Christmas Emergency!

Zoe Parker looked at the twinkly lights hanging around the room and gave a happy sigh. Christmas was her favourite holiday, but this year it was going to be even more special. This year, her friend Talia and her mum had come to stay. Talia's mum, Katie, and Zoe's mum, Lucy, had been best friends since they were little.

"Do you think anyone's ever made an advent calendar for a red panda before?" asked Zoe, carefully cutting a door in the front of a large cardboard box. On the floor beside her were a pile of apples, bamboo and pieces of corn bread to hide behind the doors.

"I don't think so," giggled Talia. "Do you think anyone's ever made a monkey a cuddly snowman?" She held up the toy snowman she'd been making.

"Definitely not," laughed Zoe. "But I know the monkeys are going to love it!"

"Spending Christmas in a zoo is the best!" exclaimed Talia as she put the finishing touches to the snowman's face.

Zoe grinned. Thanks to her Great-Uncle Horace, she got to spend every

Christmas in a zoo because she lived in the Rescue Zoo that he owned. Great-Uncle Horace was a famous explorer and animal expert. He'd created the Rescue Zoo as a safe place for animals who were endangered, lost or hurt. Zoe and her mum lived in a cottage in the zoo because Lucy was the zoo vet.

Zoe started painting a robin on the advent calendar door. She had asked her Great-Uncle Horace if she and Talia could come to his house, Higgins Hall, to make some Christmas treats for the zoo animals. The girls were sitting in front of the large fireplace in Great-Uncle Horace's living room. A fire was crackling away in the hearth and paints, cardboard and pieces of fruit covered the rug all around them.

Zoe's mouse lemur, Meep, waved his paws as he looked at the fruit. His long grey tail bobbed up and down with excitement.

"Can I have a treat? Can I have a treat?" he chattered.

"I wonder what Meep's saying," said Talia.

"I wonder." Zoe smiled. The truth was, she knew exactly what Meep was saying because Zoe had a very special secret. Ever since she was six years old, she'd been able to understand animals – and they could understand her too. No one else knew her secret, not even her mum or Great-Uncle Horace. Zoe had to be very careful not to give it away.

"I think he must be getting excited for Christmas," she said. She stroked the little

mouse lemur's silky fur. "Don't worry,
Meep, it's only three days until Christmas.
Santa will come late on Christmas Eve
and then you'll have loads of treats in
your stocking."

Meep scampered
over to the
fireplace
where three
stockings
were
hanging
from the
mantelpiece.
One for Zoe,
one for Meep, and
one for Talia. They were
gifts from Great-Uncle Horace
to hang in Zoe's house on Christmas Eve.

"Do you think Santa will give me a banana?" chirped Meep.

Zoe waited until Talia wasn't looking and nodded. "I'm sure he will," she whispered.

"What colour hat shall I give the – the – ACHOO!" Talia let out a huge sneeze, causing Meep to jump.

"Bless you!" giggled Zoe.

"Thank you." Talia sniffed. "What colour hat shall I give the snowman?"

"How about red?" suggested Zoe, as she coloured in the robin.

"Good idea!" Talia grinned. "Wouldn't it be cool if it snowed by Christmas Day? Then we could make a real snowman."

"That would be great," agreed Zoe.

The big old grandfather clock in the corner of the room began to strike and

Meep jerked again, then snuggled in next to Zoe.

"It's going to be so much fun giving our Christmas treats to the animals," said Talia.

"Can I have some? Pretty please?" chattered Meep.

Talia laughed. "Meep's so funny. It's like he's trying to join in with our conversation."

"Yes," said Zoe, patting Meep on the head. If only Talia knew he really was joining in!

"I can't wait till we dress up as elves tomorrow." Talia cut a hat shape out of red felt.

"Me too," said Zoe.

Great-Uncle Horace had asked the girls if they'd dress up as elves for the Rescue

Zoo's Christmas celebration the next day. He was going to dress up as Santa and the girls were going to help the zoo visitors have their photos taken with him.

"I love our costumes," said Talia. "They're so – so – ACHOO!"

Meep jumped again. "Why does she keep sneezing?" he chirped to Zoe.

But before Zoe could say anything, the phone started to ring. Like most of the things in Great-Uncle Horace's house, the phone was very old-fashioned. You had to move the phone's dial in a circle instead of pressing the numbers to make a call. It was very loud too.

Great-Uncle Horace hurried into the room. His white beard was longer than ever. He'd been growing it to make him look more like Santa. A beautiful bright-blue macaw flew in after him. It was Kiki, Great-Uncle Horace's pet who went everywhere with him. She perched on top of the grandfather clock and fluffed up her feathers.

"Hello, girls, hello, Meep," said Great-Uncle Horace, before picking up the receiver. "Good morning, Higgins Hall, Horace Higgins speaking," he boomed. His smile faded as he listened to the caller. "Oh dear," he said. "Oh dear, dear, dear."

Zoe and Talia exchanged worried glances.

"I'll be there straight away," said Great-Uncle Horace before putting the receiver down.

"What's happened?" asked Zoe.

"There's been a Christmas emergency," replied Great-Uncle Horace. "A family of animals need a home. I need to tell Mr Pinch to get ready for some new arrivals. I'll see you girls later." He hurried from the room.

Talia turned to Zoe, her eyes shining.

"Wow, new animals arriving! Isn't that amazing?"

Zoe started to smile. "It feels like the best Christmas present ever!"

Chapter Two
Clicking Hooves

That afternoon, Zoe and Talia waited by the Rescue Zoo gates, eagerly looking for any sign of Great-Uncle Horace coming down the road.

"I wonder which animals he's had to rescue this time," said Zoe.

"I hope it's something unusual," said Talia. "I hope he has – ACHOO!"

"I hope he has a tissue too," chattered Meep, swinging from the carved animals on the top of the zoo gates, "to give to sneezy Talia!"

Zoe had to bite her lip to stop herself laughing. "Bless you – again!" she said to Talia. "I hope you're not catching a cold."

Talia's face fell. "I hope not. I'd hate to get ill at Christmas!"

"I hope Great-Uncle Horace has rescued a family of animals who like fruit," chattered Meep. "And who like to share their fruit too – especially with mouse lemurs."

"Here he comes!" cried Zoe, as she spotted Great-Uncle Horace's jeep coming along the road. "He's pulling the horse trailer."

"Ooh, do you think he's rescued some

horses?" asked Talia. "I love horses."

As the jeep got closer, Zoe's skin tingled with excitement. And as Great-Uncle Horace drove through the gates, she saw something that made her even more excited, poking out of the window in the horse box.

"Look, look!" cried Zoe. "I can see an antler!"

"Do animals with antlers like fruit?" chirped Meep, scampering down from the gate.

14

"I'm not sure, but we'll soon find out," whispered Zoe as she crouched down to pick him up.

"Hello girls," said Great-Uncle Horace, as he got out of the jeep. "Allow me to introduce you to the newest residents of the Rescue Zoo." He opened the door at the back of the horsebox and a huge pair of antlers appeared, followed by the most beautiful reindeer Zoe had ever seen. Its coat was white and grey, and its eyes were black and shiny.

"This is Dasher," said Great-Uncle Horace, patting the large reindeer on the back. "He's the father of the family. And this is Dancer, the mum."

Another reindeer came down from the horsebox. She was almost as big as Dasher and her fur was brown, with white patches on her face. As she trotted on to the ground Zoe heard a clicking sound that seemed to be coming from Dancer's feet.

"What's that noise?" asked Zoe.

"Aha!" beamed Great-Uncle Horace. "All reindeers' hooves make a clicking

sound when they move. It can be very helpful when they're in a snowstorm as the other reindeer in the herd are able to hear where they are."

"That's so clever," said Talia.

"I wish my paws made a clicking sound," chattered Meep, scampering up on to Zoe's shoulder. "How would you find me if I got lost in a snowstorm?"

"Luckily, you have a very noisy mouth," whispered Zoe with a giggle.

"This is their oldest calf," said Great-Uncle Horace, as a much smaller reindeer with much smaller antlers came out of the horse box. "His name is Comet." Great-Uncle Horace stroked the calf's head.

"He's so cute!" exclaimed Talia.

"And this is Comet's sister," said Great-

Uncle Horace, as a little fawn-coloured reindeer with white patches came out of the trailer on wobbly legs. Her antlers were so tiny, they were even smaller than her ears!

"I wonder what her name is," said Talia. "Maybe she's Prancer."

"Or she could be Blitzen," replied Zoe.

"She's actually called Raina," said Great-Uncle Horace.

"Oh," said Talia. "I wonder why she doesn't have a traditional reindeer name."

"It's a lovely name though," said Zoe, "and she's so beautiful. Where did you rescue them from?"

"They were in a Christmas fair," explained Great-Uncle Horace. "The owners didn't really know how to take care of reindeer, so they asked if I'd provide them with a home here instead."

"This is a great Christmas surprise!" exclaimed Zoe.

"I hate surprises," a voice muttered.

Zoe turned to see Mr Pinch, the zoo

manager, standing behind her. He was dressed very smartly in his uniform, and his polished shoes gleamed in the wintery sun.

"Why do you hate surprises?" asked Zoe.

"Because they usually involve a mess of one kind or another." Mr Pinch frowned as the reindeer started grazing on the grass beside them. "See, they've already started to chew up my neatly mown lawn."

"Don't worry, Mr Pinch," said Great-Uncle Horace with a smile. "We'll soon have them in their new home." He turned to Zoe and Talia. "Would you girls like to help me get them settled?"

"Of course!" exclaimed Zoe.

"Yes please!" cried Talia.

Great-Uncle Horace took some rope from the jeep and made them into leads for each of the reindeer.

"I'll take the big 'uns," he said, "And you can take the little 'uns." He gave Talia Comet's lead and passed Raina's lead to Zoe.

Zoe stroked Raina's fur. "Welcome to the Rescue Zoo," she whispered in her ear. Raina gave a friendly grunt in reply.

Great-Uncle Horace led them through the zoo to a field next to the llamas' enclosure. The field had been kept wild and was full of evergreens. Tony, the llamas' keeper, came hurrying over.

"Hello, Horace, hello Zoe," he said.

"Hello, Tony," replied Zoe. "This is my friend Talia. She's staying with me for Christmas."

"Will the reindeer be all right living out here in the cold?" asked Talia with a shiver.

"Don't worry," replied Tony. "Reindeers love the cold."

Raina grunted and nuzzled up to Zoe.

"Apparently, reindeer have two coats to

keep them warm," said Zoe.

Raina grunted again.

"They have a nice soft undercoat, and a topcoat of longer, stiffer hairs."

"Wow, how do you know so much, Zoe?" asked Talia.

"Oh, I – uh – read it in a book," Zoe stammered. She could hardly tell Talia that Raina had told her!

"The reindeers are going to make such a great addition to our Christmas celebration," said Great-Uncle Horace. "We'll have to move our Santa's grotto here beside the enclosure so the visitors can see them. They'll be just like Santa's real reindeer."

"They even have the same names as Santa's reindeer," said Talia with a sniff. "Well, apart from Raina."

Raina's head fell and her tail drooped.

"The Christmas celebration is going to be so cool!" exclaimed Zoe.

But Mr Pinch scowled. "More visitors making more mess," he muttered.

As they led the reindeer into the field to let them explore their new home, Zoe noticed that Raina didn't look as happy as the others.

"Are you all right?" she whispered.

Raina nuzzled her head against Zoe and gave a low bark.

"Oh, I'm sure you won't get your new antlers tangled in something," replied Zoe.

Raina gave a worried neigh.

"It doesn't matter that you don't have a Christmassy name," replied Zoe. "I bet you'll be great at being a Christmas reindeer!"

Comet came over with Meep riding on his back. He nudged Raina playfully and barked.

"Hey, don't say that to your sister," called Zoe.

"What did he say?" asked Meep.

"He said that Raina's so clumsy she'd better be careful not to knock Santa over," replied Zoe.

Raina hung her head and gave a sad yelp.

Comet barked again.

"Don't worry, he's just teasing," said Zoe. "You won't really knock him over."

Comet nuzzled his sister.

"There, see? He didn't mean it," said Zoe kindly.

Raina gave a doubtful grunt.

"Of course being part of the Christmas celebration will be fun," said Zoe, patting the little reindeer on the head. She looked around for Talia and saw her leaning against the fence, shivering.

"Are you OK, Talia?" Zoe asked,

hurrying over. "You look really pale."

Talia gave another loud sneeze. "Oh, Zoe, I think I really might be getting ill. My head hurts and I can't stop shivering."

"Maybe it's just the cold," said Zoe. "I bet once you get back inside you'll feel OK."

But as the two girls headed back out of the field, Zoe couldn't help worrying. Talia getting ill would be a serious Christmas emergency!

Chapter Three
Jingle Bells

The next morning Zoe woke up bright and early, excited for the Rescue Zoo's Christmas celebration.

"I can't wait to dress up as an elf," she said to Meep, taking her green and red elf's dress out of the wardrobe.

"I can't wait to have breakfast," chirped Meep, jumping down from his cushion at the end of Zoe's bed.

"You have to put your costume on first," said Zoe. She rummaged in her wardrobe and pulled out a little green pointed hat with a bell on the end and a tiny strip of elastic to hold it in place. "Don't fidget," she said, as she carefully placed the hat on the little mouse lemur's head.

"I always fidget when I'm hungry," said Meep. "Thinking about blueberries makes my tummy really excited."

Zoe laughed as she secured the elastic. "Oh Meep, you're the sweetest elf I've ever seen!" she exclaimed.

While Zoe put her own costume on, Meep scampered over to the mirror. As soon as he saw his reflection, he started running round in a circle, causing the bell on his hat to jingle.

"Now that I've got a jingly hat, you'll always be able to find me," he chirped.

Zoe laughed and picked him up. "Come on, let's see if Talia's awake. I hope she's feeling better today." Zoe popped Meep on to her shoulder and went into the spare room. Talia was still fast asleep, buried under her duvet. "Wake up, sleepy head," called Zoe. "It's breakfast time."

Meep scampered on top of Talia and started jumping up and down. "My jingly bell will wake her up," he chattered excitedly.

Talia groaned from beneath her duvet.

"What's wrong?" asked Zoe.

"I don't feel well," mumbled Talia. "I kept coughing in the night, and now I feel really hot."

"Oh no!" cried Zoe. "Let me go and get my mum. She might have some medicine to make you feel better."

Zoe ran downstairs with Meep scampering behind her.

"Something terrible has happened," she announced, bursting into the kitchen.

Zoe's mum, Lucy, was standing at the oven making pancakes and Talia's mum, Katie, was pouring a pot of coffee into a cup.

Lucy spun round, a pancake dropping off the spatula she was holding. "What is it?" she gasped.

"What's wrong?" asked Katie.

"Talia won't get out of bed," replied Zoe. "She says she's not feeling well, but if she's ill she'll miss the Christmas celebration! Do you have any medicine you can give her, Mum?" As a vet, Lucy was great at making sick animals feel better. Zoe only hoped she could do the same for Talia.

"Let's go and see," said Lucy, picking up the dropped pancake and putting it in the bin.

They all went back upstairs. Talia was still buried beneath her duvet.

"What's wrong, love?" asked Katie, crouching down beside the bed.

"My throat hurts and I keep coughing and I'm really hot," muttered Talia, poking her head out.

"Oh dear," said Lucy. She put her hand on Talia's forehead. "I'm afraid you have a fever."

"Oh no!" said Zoe.

"ACHOO!" Talia sneezed. "Does this mean I won't be able to be an elf?" she sniffed.

"I'm afraid so," said Katie.

"The best place for you today is right here in bed," said Lucy.

Zoe felt so sad for her friend that she wanted to cry. "Well, if you're not going to be able to be an elf then I won't be one either," she said. "I'll stay here and keep you company."

But Katie shook her head. "That's very kind of you, Zoe, but Talia needs to rest."

"It's OK, Zoe," said Talia. "You and Meep go and help Great-Uncle Horace while I get some sleep."

"Are you sure?" Zoe looked at Talia.

Talia nodded sadly.

"Do you want to borrow any of my books?" asked Zoe. "Or watch a movie on my tablet?"

"No thanks," said Talia. "I just want to sleep."

"OK," said Zoe. She really hoped Talia would feel better after she'd had some rest.

After a quick breakfast, Zoe and Meep set off to help Great-Uncle Horace. When she got to the gate of the cottage, she turned and saw Talia watching her from the spare bedroom window. Zoe waved at her sadly.

Zoe made her way along the winding path through the zoo with Meep perched on her shoulder. Just like Meep's hat, the pointy toes of her shoes had bells on them. Every time they walked past an enclosure the animals would come hurrying over at the jingly sound.

As they walked past the kangaroo enclosure, Bouncer the kangaroo came bounding over and yelped with delight when he saw Zoe and Meep.

"We're dressed as Christmas elves," Zoe explained with a giggle. She wiggled her feet and Meep shook his head to make their bells jingle louder. Bouncer hopped along.

The next enclosure they came to
belonged to the giraffes. The youngest
giraffe, Jamie, bent his long neck down
to see what was making the noise. He
whinnied excitedly when he saw Zoe and
Meep's costumes.

"I love being an elf," Meep chattered as they continued on their way. "It makes everyone happy."

Zoe nodded. Even though she was still sad about Talia being ill, wearing the elf costume had cheered her up too. When they reached the reindeers' new enclosure, her happiness grew. Great-Uncle Horace and some of the zookeepers had moved Santa's grotto right next to the field. Dasher, Dancer, Raina and Comet were grazing alongside it. A brightly painted sign above the grotto door said: VISIT SANTA AND HIS REINDEER TODAY!

A huge Christmas tree, with a flashing star on the top and decked in colourful fairy lights, stood on one side of the grotto. On the other side was a sledge laden with gifts. As Zoe and Meep got closer, Great-Uncle Horace appeared at the door dressed in his costume. With his rosy cheeks and long white beard he looked just like Santa.

"Ho ho ho! Here are my elves," he boomed. Then he frowned and looked

around. "But where's my other helper?"

"Talia's not feeling well," said Zoe. "She's had to stay in bed."

"Oh dear, what a shame," said Great-Uncle Horace, shaking his head.

"Uh-oh!" yelped Meep, scampering up on to Zoe's shoulder. She turned to see Mr Pinch marching towards them, holding a clipboard.

"Excuse me, elf?" he called over to Zoe.

"Er, yes?" replied Zoe.

"I need you to make sure that people form an orderly queue today at this grotty –"

"Grotto," Zoe corrected.

"Hmm," Mr Pinch looked at the grotto and frowned. "I need you to make sure that people queue up neatly. There's been more than enough mess made recently."

Mr Pinch peered into the reindeers' enclosure. Just then a gust of wind blew his hat from his head. It flew through the air and landed in the enclosure. "Oh, drat!" he said.

"Don't worry, I can let you in." Zoe hurried over to the enclosure gate and felt for the silver paw print pendant around her neck. Great-Uncle Horace had given her the pendant as a birthday present and it opened all of the enclosures in the zoo.

"Thank you." Mr Pinch barged past her into the enclosure and picked up his hat. "Oh, calamity!" he exclaimed.

"What's wrong?" asked Zoe.

"There's mud all over it." As Mr Pinch marched back out of the enclosure, Zoe looked at the hat. There was one speck of mud on it, the size of a pea. "And here comes more mess," Mr Pinch grumbled as a stream of visitors started making their way along the path towards them. He looked at Zoe. "Don't forget what I said. Neat queues please."

As the visitors reached the grotto, Great-Uncle Horace came out and waved to them. "Ho, ho, ho!" he boomed. "Who wants to visit Santa and his reindeer?"

"Me, me, me!" cried the visitors.

Great-Uncle Horace went back into his grotto, and Zoe and Meep helped the visitors get into a queue. Mr Pinch walked up and down beside them, tutting every so often if someone stepped out of their place.

"Ah, look at the baby reindeer!" said a little girl as Comet and Raina nuzzled each other. Then Comet started chasing

Raina round and round in a circle. The children watching started to giggle.

"They're so cute," said one of the girls.

As Raina ran past a bush overhanging the fence, she accidentally got her little antlers tangled in the branches. The bush had been decorated with bells, so when Raina tried to pull herself free, the whole bush jingled.

The children cheered.

One little boy clapped his hands. "It's a Christmas show!" he cried.

But Zoe could see that Raina wasn't trying to put on a show at all – she was very upset. Raina tugged and tugged and finally got her antlers free. As the children carried on laughing, the little reindeer hurried towards to the gate, which suddenly flapped open in the wind.

"Oh no!" exclaimed Zoe. She poked her head inside the grotto. "Great-Uncle Horace – I mean, Santa, we've got a problem."

"What is it?" asked Great-Uncle Horace.

"A runaway reindeer!" replied Zoe, as Raina ran out of the enclosure.

The little boy sitting on Great-Uncle Horace's knee gasped.

"Don't worry, I'll be back soon," said Great-Uncle Horace. He handed the boy to his mum and quickly followed Zoe outside.

"Oh dear!" exclaimed Zoe as Raina went charging into the big Christmas tree, sending some of the decorations flying.

"Look at the mess!" cried Mr Pinch.

"This is the best Santa's grotto ever!" exclaimed a little boy as they all watched Raina running around with tinsel from the tree stuck on her antlers.

The children leapt out of the way as Raina came charging past them.

"Stay in your places!" yelled Mr Pinch. "Keep your formation!" He turned to Zoe. "Why is this animal on the loose?"

"The gate came open," replied Zoe.

"Oh no!" Mr Pinch's face fell. "I was so

worried about my hat, I forgot to close it properly behind me."

Zoe started running after Raina, with Meep scampering along beside her, their bells jingling.

"Raina, come back!" Zoe cried. But it was too late. Zoe watched in horror as Raina crashed into the sledge and tumbled into a heap on the ground.

Chapter Four
New Friends

Zoe crouched down next to the little reindeer.

"Raina, are you OK?"

Raina gave a whimper.

"The children weren't laughing at you." Zoe stroked Raina's tawny fur. "They didn't think you were silly, they thought you were fun."

"Yes, you're lots of fun," chattered Meep.

"Is she all right?" puffed Great-Uncle Horace as he came running over with Tony.

"I'm not sure," replied Zoe. "I think she might have hurt her leg. She's really trembling."

"I'm so sorry," said Mr Pinch as he hurried over. "If only I'd checked I'd shut the gate properly."

"Keeping the animals safe in their enclosures is our most important job here at the zoo," said Great-Uncle Horace. "But don't worry, Mr Pinch, I know you didn't mean to do it. Now, I think we should get this little one to the zoo hospital and have her checked over. Could you carry her, Tony?"

"Of course." Tony crouched down and

picked Raina up.

"It's all right," Zoe whispered to the little reindeer. "You're going to see my mum. She'll make sure you're OK."

Raina gave a little whimper.

"Can I go with her, Great-Uncle Horace?" asked Zoe.

"Of course." Great-Uncle Horace nodded. "You're always so good with the animals, Zoe. You'll make the perfect companion for Raina."

The zoo visitors all watched in silence as Tony carried Raina along the footpath, with Zoe and Meep following behind. Dancer, Dasher and Comet all watched from the fence of their enclosure. As Zoe walked past, Comet gave an anxious bark.

"She's hurt her leg, but don't worry,"

whispered Zoe. "My mum will help her feel better."

When they got to the hospital Lucy was in the examination room, bandaging one of Ruby the red panda's paws.

"Goodness me!" she exclaimed when she saw them. "What happened?"

"Raina ran away from her enclosure," explained Zoe. "And she crashed into the sledge and fell over. I think she might have hurt her leg."

"Let's have a look," said Lucy. "Tony, could you put her on the table?"

Tony carefully placed Raina on the examination table. Lucy started feeling the reindeer's legs. When she touched one of Raina's ankles the little reindeer yelped.

"It's all right, she hasn't broken

anything," said Lucy, stroking Raina's head. "It's just a minor sprain. She'll have to stay here for a bit and rest while it heals."

"Oh no," said Zoe. "First Talia gets poorly and now Raina's sick too!"

"Don't worry," said Lucy. "Raina won't have to stay here for long. Why don't you introduce her to some new friends while she is here?"

"Good idea!" said Zoe.

While Lucy and Tony went into the office to fill out some paperwork, Zoe gave Raina a cuddle.

Raina gave a sad little bark.

"Oh Raina, of course you belong at the zoo," Zoe replied.

Raina yelped.

"No one's mad at you for making a

mess. It wasn't your fault the gate was left open."

Raina nuzzled Zoe and gave another little bark.

"You do belong here, and now I'm going to introduce you to some new friends." She turned to Ruby. "This is Ruby the red panda. What happened to your paw, Ruby?"

The little panda grunted.

"Oh dear. Ruby cut her paw on a prickly bush," explained Zoe.

Then she went over to a bed in the corner where a little macaque monkey named Marty was curled up looking very sorry for himself.

"Why are you here, Marty?" asked Zoe. He gave a sad little yelp.

"You caught your tail on a tree?" said

55

Zoe. She turned to Raina. "There, see? You're not the only animal who's had an accident."

Raina barked
and nodded her
head happily.

Then Zoe heard
a loud squawk from
the corner. She turned
to see Great-Uncle
Horace's beautiful blue
hyacinth macaw, Kiki,
sitting on a perch.

"Kiki!" exclaimed Zoe. "What
happened? Why are you here?"

Kiki squawked again.

"Poor Kiki wasn't feeling well, so she
needs to rest and have some special
vitamin drops," Zoe told Raina. The little
reindeer nodded again. "So you might
have hurt your ankle, but you've got three
new friends," said Zoe.

As the animals began to play together, Zoe picked up Meep.

"I'm just going to go and tell your family what's happened," she said to Raina.

The little reindeer barked, then carried on playing with her new friends.

When Zoe got back to the reindeer enclosure, she found Dasher, Dancer and Comet all waiting anxiously by the fence. As soon as they saw Zoe, Comet gave a nervous bark.

Zoe ran over and patted him on the head. "It's all right. Raina has a sprained ankle and she's going to stay in the zoo hospital tonight so she can rest."

Dasher and Dancer grunted gratefully. Comet nuzzled up to Zoe and she realised he had something in his mouth. He gave a little bark.

"You've got a present for Raina?" asked Zoe.

Comet nodded and barked again.

"What is it?" asked Meep from Zoe's shoulder.

"It's a piece of lichen," replied Zoe. "Apparently it's Raina's favourite snack."

She patted Comet on the head and took the lichen. "Thank you, Comet. I bet this will make Raina really happy."

"What's lichen?" asked Meep as they made their way over to the grotto, where Mr Pinch was sweeping the footpath.

"It's a plant that grows on trees," explained Zoe.

"Yuck!" Meep shook his head.

Zoe giggled. "You might think it's yucky, Meep, but to other animals it's delicious."

"How's the reindeer?" Mr Pinch called.

"She has a sprained ankle so she's going to stay in the hospital for a while," replied Zoe.

"Oh dear." Mr Pinch stopped sweeping and leaned on his broom. "If only I'd checked the gate. I need to be more organised from now on and make sure that never happens again."

Zoe wasn't sure if it was possible for Mr Pinch to be more organised than he already was!

"Anyway, I have a treat for the little reindeer. To say I'm sorry." Mr Pinch reached inside his pocket and handed Zoe a leaf-eater biscuit.

"Thank you!" exclaimed Zoe. "She'll love it."

As Zoe set off back to her home, Meep chattered in her ear.

"Do you think Raina would mind if I had a little nibble of her biscuit? Being an elf has made me feel really hungry."

"You're always feeling really hungry," giggled Zoe. "And no, you can't have a nibble – it's Raina's present. Anyway, I don't think you'd like this kind of biscuit."

"Why not?" asked Meep.

"Because it's made for animals who love to eat leaves," explained Zoe.

"Gross!" yelped Meep, wrinkling his little nose. "Are you sure she wouldn't rather have a banana?"

Zoe laughed and shook her head. "No, this is exactly what Raina would like."

Chapter Five
Christmas Treats

As Zoe made her way along the winding path through the zoo, she saw something that made her stop in her tracks. A large figure with a long white beard, dressed in red, was walking through the twilight towards her.

"It's Santa!" she whispered to Meep.

"But isn't it too early for Santa to

come?" chirped Meep.

"Hello, Zoe," called Santa.

"Oh!" exclaimed Zoe. "It's Great-Uncle Horace."

"I knew it," said Meep.

Zoe ran over to Great-Uncle Horace and gave him a hug. "I thought you were the real Santa, you look so much like him."

"Ho, ho, ho!" laughed Great-Uncle Horace. "How's Talia doing?"

"I don't know yet, I'm just on my way to see her. I hope she's feeling better."

"I bet you'll cheer her up when you tell her all about today's adventures!" replied Great-Uncle Horace. "And if that doesn't do, why don't you give her some treats from Santa?" He winked, then reached into his pocket and pulled out a handful of sweets.

"Thank you, Great-Uncle Horace," said Zoe, taking the sweets. "These should definitely do the trick."

"See you in the morning," said Great-Uncle Horace, before continuing on his way.

"Why is everyone getting treats except for me?" chattered Meep as they walked up the garden path.

"Don't worry, I'm sure Mum has some treats for your dinner," replied Zoe.

She opened the door to the cottage. The delicious smell of baking filled the air.

"Yum!" cried Meep. "That smell is making my tummy growl like a tiger!"

"Mine too," laughed Zoe.

She hurried into the kitchen to find Lucy rolling some pastry and Katie mixing something in a bowl. A tray of cookies was cooling on the counter.

"Hello, Zoe," said Katie. "Your mum and I are making some mince pies."

"Great," said Zoe. "How's Talia?"

"She's still poorly, I'm afraid," replied Lucy. "Why don't you go and see her?"

Zoe and Meep hurried upstairs. Talia was still in bed.

"Hi, Talia." Zoe came and sat on the end of the bed, and Meep perched beside her. "How are you feeling?"

"I have a sore throat," said Talia in a croaky voice. "And I'm still really shivery."

"Do you want a treat?" asked Zoe. She put her hand in her pocket and pulled out the piece of lichen Comet had given her. "Whoops, wrong treat," she giggled. "This one's for Raina. She's in hospital," she explained. She reached into her other pocket and pulled out a handful of sweets. As Talia popped a toffee into her mouth Zoe told her all about Raina's runaway adventure.

"I can't believe that happened!" exclaimed Talia, once Zoe had finished. She leaned back and gave a big yawn.

"Poor Raina…" she closed her eyes. "I … do … hope … she … gets … better…"

"Why's she talking so slowly?" Meep chattered in Zoe's ear.

"She's falling asleep," whispered Zoe.

"But it's not bedtime," chirped Meep. "We haven't even had our dinner."

"It's because she's so poorly," whispered Zoe.

"What if she sleeps all through Christmas?" chattered Meep.

"I really hope she doesn't," sighed Zoe. "Come on, let's go and get something to eat."

They went back downstairs and into the kitchen. Meep scampered over to the table and watched eagerly as Katie and Lucy filled the pastry for the pies with the fruity mixture.

"What if Talia doesn't get well in time and she sleeps all through Christmas?" Zoe asked anxiously. "I want her to have fun, not feel poorly."

"Don't worry," said Lucy. "We'll make sure Talia has a lovely Christmas, even if she is still ill."

"Yes, we could decorate her room," said Katie.

"And we can bring her nice food and presents," said Lucy.

Zoe nodded. This plan made her feel slightly better about Talia being ill at Christmas. Then she had a great idea. Maybe she could do something nice for the poorly animals in the zoo hospital too!

Chapter Six
Going on a Food Hunt

Zoe was woken the next morning by
Meep bouncing up and down at the end
of her bed.

"Wake up, Zoe, it's Christmas Eve!" he
chirped. "It's almost time for Santa to
come. Do you think all the presents are
on his sleigh? Do you think he'll have lots
for me?"

"I'm sure he will. You have been a very good mouse lemur." Zoe sat up in bed and beamed. She loved Christmas Eve. But then she remembered what had happened the day before. She hoped that her plan to give Talia and the other animals in the hospital a lovely Christmas would work. "Let's go and see how Talia is doing," she said.

"I hope she's better now," said Meep.

But when they went into the spare room, Talia greeted them with a cough and a sneeze.

Zoe smiled at her. "Don't worry, Talia, you're still going to have a great Christmas. Meep and I are going to make sure of it."

Talia sighed. "Thanks, Zoe, but I don't see how it's going to be great if I'm stuck in bed."

"Trust me, it will be," said Zoe with a grin.

Zoe went downstairs to find Lucy coming through the door carrying a small Christmas tree.

"Morning, Zoe, I thought it would be nice to put up a Christmas tree in the zoo hospital."

"Good idea!" exclaimed Zoe. "And I could decorate it with treats for the animals who are poorly."

"That would really cheer them up," Lucy agreed.

As soon as breakfast was over, Zoe made a list of the animals in the hospital and their favourite snacks. Once she'd finished her list, Zoe put on her elf costume and put Meep in his hat.

"Right, Meep, we've got an important job to do."

"What kind of job?" chirped Meep.

"We're going on a hunt for food," replied Zoe.

"That's my favourite kind of job!" chirped Meep, licking his lips.

Zoe put on a scarf and gloves and picked up a small basket to carry the food in. Then they set off around the zoo, stopping first at Ruby's enclosure.

"Good morning, Zoe, are you excited for Christmas?" called Stephanie, the panda keeper.

"Yes, I am!" replied Zoe. "I was wondering if I could have some bamboo to make Ruby a special Christmas treat. I want to cheer her up as she's in hospital."

"What a lovely idea," replied Stephanie. She went over to the storeroom and fetched Zoe a handful of bamboo.

Zoe put it in her elf's basket and carried on her way.

"Where to next?" asked Meep, scampering along by her feet.

"Next stop, the monkey enclosure," replied Zoe.

MONKEY HOUSE

"I like monkeys, they're always silly," giggled Meep.

Sure enough, when they got to the monkey enclosure, Mickey the spider monkey was swinging through the branches, shrieking at the top of his voice.

75

"Good to see you so excited for Christmas, Mickey," laughed Zoe. "Could you help me get some treats for poor old Marty?"

Mickey scampered off and returned with some nuts and a dandelion.

"Thank you, Mickey, this will really cheer Marty up," said Zoe, putting the treats in her basket.

Mickey gave a shriek.

"Yes, I'll tell him you wish him a happy Christmas," replied Zoe.

"Where to now, Zoe?" chirped Meep.

"Now we need to get some seeds for Kiki," said Zoe. "I know, let's go to the rainforest dome. Valeria is bound to have some seeds for all the parrots that live there."

The rainforest dome was lovely and

warm after the cold outside. Valeria, the rainforest keeper, happily gave Zoe some sunflower seeds and figs.

"Do you want me to carry the fruit?" asked Meep, looking at the figs hungrily.

Zoe grinned and shook her head. "Thank you very much, but I think it's probably safer if I carry them!"

Once they'd got all the food on the list they returned to the cottage. Zoe carefully wrapped the treats in gold and red tissue and hung them on the small Christmas tree for the animals. Then she made a big star out of gold cardboard and stuck it on the top of the tree. It wasn't as fancy as the flashing star on the big tree in Santa's grotto, but it looked very pretty.

Later that afternoon, Zoe, Lucy and

Meep set off for the hospital, carefully carrying the small decorated tree between them. As they reached the hospital doors, Lucy was called away by one of the keepers. They set the tree down and Zoe went in to check on the animals. They all looked a bit sad, but as soon as they saw Zoe and Meep, Raina waved her antlers, Ruby gave a happy yelp, Marty let out a cheery shriek and Kiki whistled a jolly tune.

"Hello, everyone," Zoe said. "I've got a special Christmas surprise for you."

"A delicious surprise," chirped Meep, scampering up and down the ward excitedly.

Zoe brought in the tree and placed it in the middle of the room where all the animals could see it.

Raina's nose twitched and she gave a happy bark.

"That's right," said Zoe. "You can smell oats. I've made you a special treat and hung it on the tree for you." She pointed to one of the packages dangling from the branches.

Marty the monkey gave a happy shriek as he spotted the dandelions.

"Yes, they're for you," said Zoe.

As the other animals looked for their gifts on the tree Zoe went over to Raina. "How are you feeling today?" she asked, stroking the little reindeer.

Raina gave a happy bark and then walked slowly around Zoe.

"That's great!" exclaimed Zoe. "I'm so happy your ankle isn't hurting as much."

Raina grunted shyly.

"No, of course Comet wasn't right when he said that you were too clumsy to be a Christmas reindeer. He was just teasing," said Zoe. "It was an accident that you got hurt and you make a wonderful Christmas reindeer."

Just then the sound of bells jingling filled the air. All the animals stopped chattering and looked at the door.

"Ho, ho, ho!" boomed a voice and Great-Uncle Horace came in. He was wearing his Santa costume and carrying a sack. "Hello, everyone. I've brought you some gifts." As he started taking the gifts from his bag Zoe saw they were some of the ones she'd made with Talia.

The animals were so excited to see their presents. As Ruby started opening the doors on her advent calendar and Marty played with his toy snowman, Zoe felt in her pocket.

"I have some more gifts for you, Raina."

The little reindeer barked happily as Zoe gave her the leaf-eater biscuit.

"This is from Mr Pinch to say sorry for leaving the enclosure gate open."

Raina gobbled up the biscuit.

"And this is from Comet. He told me it was your favourite snack." Zoe held out the lichen.

Raina barked happily and ate that too.

"Right, I'd better be going," said Great-Uncle Horace. "I have a lot of other presents to deliver and it's almost evening."

The animals all barked and chirped and squawked goodbye.

As it grew darker outside, the little tree

looked even prettier.

"I know," said Zoe. "Let's all make a wish on the Christmas star." She pointed to the painted cardboard star on the top of the tree.

"I wish that Santa would fill my stocking with lots of yummy blueberries and bananas," chirped Meep.

Zoe giggled.

Kiki wished that she could be well enough to spend Christmas Day with Great-Uncle Horace. Ruby wished that she could have some snow to play in as soon as she was better. And Marty wished that he could grow a pair of wings, which made Meep fall over from laughing so much.

Zoe turned to Raina. "How about you?" she asked. "What's your Christmas wish?"

The little reindeer
gazed up at the star
on top of the tree
and gave a sad
little bark.

"Oh Raina, you didn't mess everything up!" Zoe gave her a hug. "Christmas doesn't need to be perfect to be happy."

Meep came bounding over and perched on Raina's back. "Tell Raina about the time you messed up Christmas, Zoe. That made me very happy," he giggled.

"Oh yes!" Zoe laughed. "A few years ago, I was having Christmas dinner with my Great-Uncle Horace and my mum and my auntie and uncle and cousins."

"Tell her about the disaster! Tell her about the disaster!" cried Meep.

"All right, all right," giggled Zoe. She stroked Raina on the head. "My mum asked me if I'd carry the brussels sprouts to the dinner table but just as I was coming into the dining room—"

"I love this bit!" interrupted Meep,

his tail springing up and down with excitement.

"I fell! And the brussels sprouts went flying all over the floor!" continued Zoe.

Raina gasped and gave a frightened grunt.

"No, I didn't get into trouble at all," replied Zoe. "We still had plenty of other food to eat and it was really funny trying to find all the sprouts I'd dropped."

"It was like a Christmas dinner treasure hunt," chirped Meep.

"It actually made that Christmas special," said Zoe. "Because it gave us all a funny memory. Why don't you make another wish, Raina?"

Raina looked at the star again and barked.

"What did she wish for this time?"

asked Meep.

"She wished she could make someone else's Christmas special," replied Zoe. "That's a lovely wish, Raina."

Then Zoe closed her eyes and made her own wish. "I wish that I'll be able to give Talia a great Christmas," she whispered.

Kiki let out a squawk.

"Talia's really sad that she's missed some of the Christmas celebration because she was poorly." Zoe turned to Raina. "And she's really sad that she didn't get to see you again."

Then Zoe had a great idea. "I know! What if you helped me make a special Christmas celebration for Talia? That way both of our wishes would come true."

Raina gave an excited yelp, but then she looked worried.

"I'm sure you won't mess it up," replied Zoe. "And anyway, it doesn't have to be perfect."

Zoe looked out of the window and realised it was getting really dark. "I'd better go," she said, patting Raina on the head. "But don't worry. I'll be back soon and then we can plan our special Christmas surprise!"

Chapter Seven
The Disappearing Reindeer

When Zoe got back to the cottage, she had a lovely surprise of her own. Talia was out of bed and sitting in the living room, wearing her pyjamas and a cosy dressing gown.

"Are you feeling better?" exclaimed Zoe.

"A little bit," said Talia. Her cheeks were

definitely rosier than before.

"I've been at the zoo hospital," said Zoe, sitting down beside her. "Great-Uncle Horace brought some of the presents we made for the animals. They loved them!"

Talia smiled. "I wish I could have seen them getting their gifts."

"Talking of gifts…" said Katie, coming into the room. "It's time to put up your stockings."

Meep jumped up and down excitedly, making Talia chuckle, which then made her cough.

"He's so cute," she said to Zoe in a croaking voice. "It's as if he knows what's going on."

"Yes, it really is." Zoe giggled.

Lucy came into the room with her arms full of beautifully wrapped presents.

Meep scampered over and watched as she placed the gifts beneath the Christmas tree.

"Don't worry, Meep," laughed Lucy. "There are some gifts here for you too."

Zoe and Talia hung their stockings over the fireplace.

"I can't wait till – till – ACHOO!" Talia sneezed.

"I think you might need to go back to bed, young lady," said Katie, giving Talia a hug.

"Oh!" Talia looked really sad.

"Don't worry," said Zoe. "You're going to have a great Christmas, I promise."

Talia nodded and trudged upstairs.

After dinner, Lucy came into the kitchen holding her vet's bag. "I need to check on my patients before bedtime," she said.

"Can I come too?" asked Zoe. "I'd like to check on Raina again."

"Of course. But make sure you wrap up warm," replied Lucy. "It's getting really cold out there."

Zoe put on her warmest coat and a woolly hat and gloves. She tucked Meep inside her coat to keep him warm.

When they got to the hospital, Zoe went straight over to Raina. As soon as Raina saw Zoe, she gave a happy bark.

"I'm so pleased your ankle doesn't hurt anymore!" exclaimed Zoe. "Now hopefully we'll be able to give Talia her Christmas surprise." She went over to Lucy. "Mum, can I take Raina back to her enclosure? She doesn't seem to be in pain now."

Lucy came over and checked Raina's ankle. "It really does seem a lot better," she said. "OK, you can take her back. I bet her family will be pleased to see her!"

"Thanks, Mum!" Zoe grinned with excitement. Not only was she going to take Raina home to her family, but she was about to give Talia a great Christmas surprise too!

As Zoe led Raina outside, she saw that snowflakes had started fluttering from the sky.

"Ruby's Christmas wish has come true!" she exclaimed.

"Ruby's Christmas wish is making my nose cold," cried Meep, snuggling deeper inside Zoe's coat.

"Thanks so much for agreeing to help," said Zoe, giving Raina a pat. "Talia's going to be so excited to see you."

Raina barked but Zoe wasn't listening properly, as Meep had started wriggling around. She let go of Raina's lead and opened her coat to look inside.

"What's wrong, Meep?" she asked.

The little mouse lemur poked his head out and sniffed the air.

"What's that delicious smell?" he chirped.

"What smell?" asked Zoe. She turned around and sniffed. Meep was right. The air was filled with the smell of something sweet and spicy and truly delicious.

"It smells like cookies," she said. She saw the lights from the café twinkling in the darkness. "Sally must be doing some baking in the café."

"It's making my tummy say 'feed me'!" chirped Meep.

Zoe giggled. "Oh Meep, you are funny. Can you smell it too, Raina?"

But when she turned to look at Raina there was no sign of her. The reindeer had run away again!

Chapter Eight
A Visit from Santa

Zoe looked all around her, but there was no sign of the little reindeer.

"Meep, did you see where Raina went?"

Meep was still sniffing the air. "She's right next to you, isn't she?"

"No, she's disappeared, and it's my fault because I let go of her lead." Zoe tried not to panic. There was no reason for Raina to run away again. She had to be close by. "Maybe she's gone to see her family." Zoe started hurrying off in the direction of the reindeer enclosure. "Raina, where are you?" she called.

"I think we should look in the café," said Meep, following her. "And while we look for her, we could look at the Christmas cookies too."

"I really don't think she's in the café," replied Zoe. "Don't worry, I'm sure we can get some cookies later."

"Raina!" Zoe called over and over as she made her way along the path. Snow was now swirling in the light of the old-fashioned lamps. What if the little reindeer had got lost? It was so cold and dark, she really hoped she was OK. When they got to the reindeers' enclosure, she saw a very

strange sight. The huge Christmas tree outside the enclosure had been knocked over and some of the decorations were missing. Dancer, Dasher and Comet were all grazing at the far side of the field. Zoe called them over.

"Have you seen Raina?" she asked anxiously.

Dasher grunted and Comet shook his head. They both looked really concerned. Dancer gave a worried bark.

"I'm so sorry. I was bringing her back to you and I let go of her lead. I only dropped it for a few seconds but she ran away. Where can she have got to?" Zoe looked back at the tree on the ground. "How did the big tree fall over? And why are some of the decorations missing?"

Zoe gasped. "I think I know where she

might be."

"Where? Where? Where?" cried Meep, poking his head out from her coat.

"You'll see." Zoe patted Comet on the head. "Don't worry. I'm going to find her and then I'll bring her home."

The reindeer all gave happy grunts.

Zoe raced back through the zoo. "Yes, I was right!" she cried as the cottage came into view.

Meep poked his head out. "Raina!" he chirped.

The little reindeer was standing on the grass beneath Talia's window. The flashing star from the big Christmas tree outside the reindeer enclosure was hanging from one of her antlers and some twinkling fairy lights were trailing down her back. Her fur was covered in snowflakes that were shimmering like glitter. Zoe had never seen anything so cute and Christmassy – and messy! Then she spotted Talia at the window. She was looking down at Raina with a huge smile on her face. Zoe ran over to the little reindeer.

"Raina, why did you run off? I was worried about you!"

Raina grunted cheerfully.

"Why did she run away?" asked Meep.

"She wanted to get a Christmas star for Talia," explained Zoe. "So that Talia could be as happy as she was on Christmas Eve." Zoe gave Raina a hug. "That's lovely, and look, Talia looks so happy."

They all looked up at the window, where Talia was now waving excitedly.

"She looks like she might be better!" exclaimed Zoe.

Just then she heard the crunching of snow behind her, and she turned to see Great-Uncle Horace in his Santa costume. His eyes were more twinkly than ever, and his smile was even more jolly. He looked so much like Santa that it gave Zoe a floaty feeling in her tummy.

"Thank you for finding my little reindeer," his voice boomed. "I have a special gift for you and your friend."

"Thank you!" exclaimed Zoe as Great-Uncle Horace gave her a beautiful red velvet bag.

"Happy Christmas!" said Great-Uncle Horace.

Zoe opened the bag. Inside were two beautiful silver Christmas tree ornaments in the shape of reindeer. "Oh wow!" she exclaimed. "Look, Raina." She took one of the silver reindeer from the bag and showed it to her. "Thank you so – oh, where did Great-Uncle Horace go?" She looked all around but there was no sign of him.

Raina barked happily at the tree ornament and Zoe put it back in the bag. There was another crunching sound on the snow and Zoe saw Great-Uncle Horace hurrying along the footpath. Zoe frowned. He was wearing his ordinary clothes.

"How could he have got changed so fast?" she whispered.

Meep's eyes widened. "Zoe, do you think that was the real Santa that we saw?"

Zoe shivered with excitement.

"Good evening, Zoe," said Great-Uncle

Horace. "What are you all doing out so late?"

"Raina and I were giving Talia a Christmas surprise," explained Zoe.

"That's wonderful!" said Great-Uncle Horace. "But Santa must be nearly here. Quick, quick, it's time to get Raina back to her family so you can all be in bed when he arrives!"

Zoe smiled to herself. She had the strangest feeling that Santa had already been!

Chapter Nine
Christmas Wishes Come True

As Great-Uncle Horace hurried off, Meep stuck his head out of Zoe's coat.

"Can I ride on Raina on the way back?" he asked. "I want to pretend that I'm Santa."

"Would that be OK?" Zoe asked Raina. The little reindeer nodded.

Zoe carefully took Meep from her

coat and placed him on Raina's back.
The little mouse lemur looked very cute
surrounded by the fairy lights.

They set off through the snow and
as they reached the elephant enclosure,
Bertie came trotting over to the fence and
trumpeted loudly.

Zoe laughed. "Raina, when he saw
you, he thought Santa had come!" she
explained.

Raina gave a proud bark.

"Don't worry Bertie, Santa will be here
really soon," Zoe called.

Next, they went past the giraffes'
enclosure. Jewel stretched her long neck
over the fence and gave a happy snort.

"She says you look very Christmassy,"
Zoe said to Raina, giving her a pat.

Raina trotted along proudly. She

seemed to become more confident with every step.

When they got to the monkey enclosure the trees came alive as the monkeys swung through the branches, chattering excitedly.

"Happy Christmas to you too!" Zoe called back.

As they reached the kangaroo enclosure, Bouncer came bounding over, chirping loudly.

"He wants to know where you got your decorations from," Zoe giggled to Raina. "He's a very curious kangaroo!"

Raina grunted merrily.

"They were a Christmas surprise," Zoe called back with a grin.

Zoe hugged Raina as they carried on their way. "Your wish has definitely come true," she said to the little reindeer. "You've made everyone's Christmas really special."

Finally, they reached the reindeers' enclosure. Dancer, Dasher and Comet barked with delight when they saw Raina. Comet was so excited he ran round and round in a circle.

"You're right, Comet," said Zoe, "Raina *is* the most Christmassy reindeer ever!"

Meep hopped down from Raina's back.
Zoe carefully untangled the decorations
from the little reindeer's antlers. Then she
wound the fairy lights around the fence
and stuck the star on top of the gate.

"Now you have some Christmas
decorations of your own," she said,
patting Raina on the head.

Zoe opened the gate with her silver
paw print pendant and let Raina in. The
other reindeers gathered around, nuzzling
her to welcome her home.

Comet barked at his sister as he pressed
his nose to her neck.

"Aw, that's nice," Zoe whispered to
Meep. "Comet says he missed her and he's
proud of her. He thinks she makes a great
Christmas reindeer."

Raina joyfully barked back and the two

young reindeer bounded off to the other side of enclosure.

Zoe laughed. "Raina says the last one to the fence is a melted snowman!" She tucked Meep back inside her coat and left the enclosure, double checking to make sure the gate was definitely locked behind her. "Good night! See you in the morning – Christmas Day morning!" she called, beaming.

As she and Meep set off along the footpath through the swirling snow, Zoe felt so happy. Thanks to Raina, it was turning out to be a truly magical Christmas. She hoped the next animal that came to the zoo would be as sweet as the little reindeer!

If you enjoyed Raina's story,
look out for:

The Talkative Tiger

Amelia Cobb

Chapter One
Very Special Guests

Zoe Parker took a fish from her bucket and threw it into the water. It was breakfast time at the Rescue Zoo where she lived, and Zoe was helping to feed the sea otters. Sasha, one of the youngest sea otters, caught the fish in her front paws and started to eat. Sasha's brother and sister, Alex and Nina, whistled happily as

Zoe threw more fish into the water for them.

Someone wasn't excited though.

"Yuck, yuck, yuck!" said Zoe's pet mouse lemur, Meep.

Zoe was able to understand what Meep was saying because Zoe had a special secret. She was able to talk to animals and understand what they were saying. No-one else knew her secret, not even her mum or her Great-Uncle Horace. "What's wrong?" she asked, crouching down beside Meep.

"Fish for breakfast!" Meep wrinkled his tiny black nose.

"Don't worry," Zoe smiled. "I have something I know you'll like." She took a banana from the pocket of her shorts, peeled it, and handed it to Meep.

"Yum, yum, yum!" exclaimed Meep, before taking a bite.

Zoe looked back at the pool. Three sea otters were floating on their backs eating their fish, their wet coats glistening in the summer sunshine.

"How are you getting on, Zoe?" Jess, the sea otters' keeper, called as she came into the enclosure.

"Great!" replied Zoe. "They're really enjoying their fish."

"They certainly seem happy," said Jess as the sea otters gave a contented cooing sound. "But are you sure you don't mind working on the first day of your summer holiday?"

"No, it's fun!" Zoe wanted to be a zookeeper when she grew up, and she loved helping with the animals whenever she could.

"It looks as if we'll be needing your help," said Jess, nodding to the empty enclosure next door. "I wonder who our new arrival will be."

Zoe looked at the enclosure. Her Great-Uncle Horace, who owned the Rescue Zoo, had recently had a beautiful new habitat built. There was a pond in the middle, with rocks and trees all around it. "It must be something that needs a lot of space and likes to climb and swim," said Zoe. "Maybe it's a crocodile!"

"Could be. Or maybe it's a family of apes," said Jess, throwing more fish into the water.

Zoe nodded.

A cheery BEEP BEEP BEEP rang out around the zoo. Great-Uncle Horace's convertible car drove through the zoo gates. The car's top was down and Great-Uncle Horace was wearing a hat to shield his face from the sun. A small trailer was attached to the back of the convertible car, holding a large crate. Zoe's heart pounded with excitement. It must be the new animal!

Zoe's Rescue Zoo

**Look out for more
amazing animal adventures
at the Rescue Zoo!**

The Rescue Princesses

Look out for another AMAZING series from Nosy Crow!

Friendship, animals and secret royal adventures!